THIS BOOK BELONGS TO:

Published by Scholastic Australia in 2023.

Scholastic Australia Pty Limited
PO Box 579 Gosford NSW 2250
ABN 11 000 614 577
www.scholastic.com.au

Part of the Scholastic Group
Sydney • Auckland • New York • Toronto • London • Mexico City • New Delhi
Hong Kong • Buenos Aires • Puerto Rico

ISBN 978-1-76026-275-4

Printed in China.

Scholastic Australia's policy, in association with its printers, is to use papers that are renewable and made efficiently from wood grown in responsibly managed forests, so as to minimise its environmental footprint.

Disney

DELUXE TREASURY

STORIES to read with DAD

SCHOLASTIC
SYDNEY AUCKLAND NEW YORK TORONTO LONDON MEXICO CITY
NEW DELHI HONG KONG BUENOS AIRES PUERTO RICO

CONTENTS

Disney Bunnies

A Day with Papa

By

KITTY RICHARDS

Illustrated by

LORI TYMINSKI & VALERIA TURATI

Thumper was terribly excited. He and his dad were spending the day together, just the two of them.

'Papa and I are going to have some great adventures in the forest,' he told his sisters.

Thumper wondered what Papa had planned. Maybe they would climb a mountain . . .

or explore a cave . . .

'I thought we'd gather some greens for supper,' Papa Bunny said. 'Remember, eating greens is a special treat. It makes long ears—and great big feet!'

'Yes, Papa,' said Thumper, his heart sinking.

Thumper and Papa got straight to work.

A little while later, Thumper wanted a nice, cool drink.

'Don't dawdle,' said Papa Bunny.

'I won't, Papa,' replied Thumper. And off he went.

While Thumper had some water, he saw ducks splashing near a waterfall.

He wished he could join them.

But Thumper knew that Papa was waiting.

He hadn't hopped very far when he saw the frogs playing.

Ribbit, ribbit!

That sure seemed like fun!

Then Thumper remembered Papa, hard at work.

After a few more hops, Thumper saw his friend, the opossum.

'Want to climb this tree with me?' the opossum asked.

'Okay!' Thumper said, forgetting about his papa.

With a little boost from his friend, Thumper was soon exploring the old oak tree.

The two peered into a bird's nest.

Chirp, Chirp.

They woke up
a sleepy owl.
Whoooooooooo!

They got close,
but not *too* close,
to a buzzing beehive.
Bzz, bzz.

‘Well, it’s time for me to go,’ the opossum said after a while. ‘My father is waiting for me.’

Uh-oh! Thumper remembered his own papa.

Thumper looked down. The ground was very far away.

How would he ever get down?

As Thumper waited, a little squirrel came by. 'Well, hello there, Thumper,' she said. 'Why don't you use your claws to get down?'

But Thumper didn't have claws.

Thumper sighed. 'Only one person can help me,' he said.

'*Whooo?*' asked the owl.

'My papa,' said Thumper sadly.

'I thought you'd never ask!' said a voice from down below. 'I've been looking for you everywhere.'

'Papa?' Thumper asked hopefully.

'Yes, Thumper, it's me,' Papa Bunny replied. 'Now take a deep breath and look down.'

Thumper opened his eyes. His papa was reaching for him.

The ground looked a lot closer now. Thumper reached down and his father pulled him into a tight hug.

'You must never be afraid to ask me for help. I am your father and I will always be here for you,' Papa Bunny said.

'I know, Papa,' said Thumper.

‘Well, all work and no play makes for a bored little bunny!’ said Papa. ‘Why don’t we race back to the meadow? Then we’ll explore a hidden cave. The last one there is a slowpoke!’

That night, the bunnies ate fresh greens. Everyone agreed they were oh-so-tasty.

'Did you have lots of adventures?' Tessie asked.
'Why, yes,' boasted Thumper. 'I even climbed a tree!'
'Oh, my,' said Daisy. 'Were you scared?'

'What a silly question,' Trixie scoffed. 'Thumper is never scared.'

Thumper looked at his dad, who gave him a big wink. Thumper grinned. He was glad he'd gotten to spend the day with his papa.

Disney

THE LION KING

A Prince's Day

By

DISNEY BOOK GROUP

Illustrated by

THE DISNEY STORYBOOK ARTISTS

It was early morning at Pride Rock. Simba and Nala couldn't wait to go out and play. 'Let's go down to the river!' Nala said loudly.

'Shhh,' Simba whispered. 'We have to be quiet or Zazu will hear us.'

But it was too late. Zazu had been on the lookout for the young prince.

'Ahh! There you are, Simba,' Zazu said, landing in front of Simba. 'Come along. We have a busy day of training ahead of us.'

'But Nala and I were about to go down to the river!' Simba complained.

'Nonsense,' Zazu said. 'As a prince you have certain responsibilities, young sire. And we can't keep them waiting.'

'Bye, Simba!' Nala said. 'Have fun at prince school! Maybe we can go to the river tomorrow.'

'Not if Zazu has anything to say about it,' Simba grumbled, watching as Nala bounded away.

Zazu led Simba down to the watering hole, where the animals of the Pride Lands were taking turns drinking water. 'Part of a ruler's responsibilities is solving disputes between his subjects.

'A perfect example is the watering hole! Each animal needs to have a turn to drink,' Zazu explained.

'See that herd of antelopes? They have been here too long. It's the rhinos' turn!'

'You! You there!' Zazu said, yelling at the antelopes.

Simba listened for what felt like hours as Zazu talked on and on to the antelopes.

Finally, the lion cub saw a chance to escape. A herd of giraffes was leaving the watering hole. If he could sneak out with them, he might still have time to play with Nala!

Just when Simba thought he had gotten away, Zazu landed in front of him.

'And where do you think you're going?' Zazu demanded.

'Come on, Zazu. We've been at the watering hole for hours. Can't I go play with Nala?' Simba asked.

But Zazu refused to let him go. 'A prince's job is never done!' he insisted. 'Onwards to our next stop!'

Zazu led Simba back to Pride Rock, where Mufasa was listening to his subjects' concerns.

'A king must listen to all the other animals,' Zazu explained. 'You can learn a lot from your father.'

Simba tried to pay attention. He listened as Mufasa advised the elephants to find new grazing grounds.

He listened as the zebras worried about the upcoming rainy season.

But soon the lion cub was just as bored as he had been at the watering hole. He started to fall asleep.

'Young sire!' Zazu yelled, angrily pecking Simba awake. 'Were you paying any attention at all?' Simba yawned, shaking himself awake. He looked around. The other animals were gone. Mufasa must have finished for the day.

'Um, I heard some of it?' Simba replied. Frustrated, Zazu flew up in the air. 'Come along, Simba. We aren't finished yet,' Zazu said.

Simba slowly followed as the bird led him away from Pride Rock. Soon they were walking past the river where Simba and Nala had planned to play that day.

Simba looked for his friend, but he didn't see her.

Suddenly, Simba heard a yell. 'Did you hear that, Zazu?' he asked.

'Hear what?' Zazu said.

There was another yell. 'That!' Simba said, running towards the river. Zazu flew after him.

It was Nala. She had fallen into the fast-moving river and couldn't get out!

'Hurry, go get my father!' Simba ordered Zazu.

The bird flew away in search of Mufasa, but Simba knew there wasn't time to wait. Nala needed him now!

Simba looked everywhere for a way to get to his best friend. Finally, he saw a long tree branch on the bank of the river.

'Nala! Grab on!' Simba yelled. He grabbed the tree branch in his mouth and moved it over the river. Nala reached out and grabbed the branch just in time!

Simba pulled the branch
back and dragged Nala out
of the river.
She was safe!

'Simba? Simba!' Mufasa called, running to the river.
'Here, Dad!' Simba said, panting. 'It's okay! I got Nala!'
Relieved, Mufasa and Zazu gathered the cubs and started back to Pride Rock.

'Zazu, Nala, can you give me a moment with Simba?' Mufasa asked. Simba was worried. Was Mufasa angry at him for not paying attention to Zazu?

'Zazu told me about your day. I know that you want to play with your friend, but Zazu was trying to teach you important lessons about what it means to be king,' Mufasa said.

'What did you learn at the watering hole?' Mufasa asked.

'That the rhinos follow the antelopes?' Simba replied.

Mufasa laughed. 'No, that you have to be fair as a ruler and make sure all your subjects are treated equally,' he said. 'And Zazu brought you to Pride Rock to show you that a leader must be wise as well. But the last lesson you taught yourself.'

'I did?' Simba said.

'Yes, my son. You rescued Nala and showed that a ruler must be brave. I am very proud of you, Simba.' Simba smiled up at his father.

'Now,' Mufasa said, 'I think there may just be enough time for you and Nala to play before dinner.'

Simba smiled and bounded off to find Nala.

'He'll make a good king someday, sire,' Zazu said, landing on Mufasa's shoulder.

Mufasa smiled. 'Yes, he will.'

Disney · PIXAR

FINDING NEMO

Night Games

By

BROOKE VITALE & ELIZABETH RUDNICK

Illustrated by

DISNEY STORYBOOK ARTISTS

Nemo and Pearl are playing tag. The friends race through the reef, darting around coral branches and tufts of seaweed.

First, Pearl is 'it'. She tags Nemo then speeds away. Now, Nemo is 'it'. He swims after her, chasing Pearl around some large rocks.

Nemo sees something scary. He suddenly forgets their game. 'Look Pearl!' Nemo points his fin at the shadowy area ahead of them.

'What *IS* that?' Pearl wonders.

The pair slowly approach the unfamiliar part of the reef.

Nemo swims even closer and peers at it. 'I think it's a giant seaweed bed!' he exclaims.

'Should we go in?' Pearl wonders.

Nemo wants to go explore the big seaweed bed, but it is getting dark. Nemo knows his dad is waiting for him to get home.

Marlin greets Nemo when he gets home. He asks Nemo about his day then tucks his son into bed.

Nemo tries to get to sleep. He counts dolphins. He tells himself a bedtime story. He even does a tricky maths problem.

It's no use! Nemo cannot fall asleep. He keeps thinking about the big seaweed bed.

What lies inside the seaweed bed? Is there treasure in there? Why is it so dark? Nemo is too curious to get to sleep.

Nemo gets out of bed and goes to find Marlin. 'Dad! Dad! Please, can we go explore the seaweed bed?' Nemo explains how curious he is, and claims that he won't be able to go to sleep until he explores it.

Eventually, Marlin agrees to go explore the seaweed bed with Nemo. But, it's too dark out. They cannot find it.

'It must be around here somewhere,' Nemo insists. 'Pearl and I were playing near these big rocks.'

Suddenly, they see a strange light approaching them.

It is a fish! The fish is glowing in the dark, lighting up the coral, seaweed and rocks around them.

‘Hello!’ Nemo calls out. ‘My name is Nemo. I like your glow!’

The mysterious fish smiles and approaches them. ‘Hello, my name is Lumen,’ she smiles at them. ‘I live here, in the seaweed bed.’

'Do you want to play hide-and-seek with me, Nemo?' Lumen asks.

Nemo quickly agrees. He is excited to play in the seaweed bed with his new friend.

Lumen takes Nemo and Marlin to the edge of the seaweed bed.

The two young fish begin to play together. Lumen tells Nemo that he is 'it', and darts away over the rocks to hide in a bed of coral. Nemo covers his eyes with his fins and starts to count to ten.

Marlin wants to explore the seaweed, so that he can make sure it's a safe place for his son to play.

He tells Nemo to stay where he is.

Marlin swims into the big seaweed bed. It is very dark in there, with large and tangling strands of seaweed blocking Marlin's view. Soon, Marlin cannot find his way out. He is lost and cannot reach Nemo!

Marlin sees a light through the thick wall of seaweed. He hurries to swim towards the glow.

It is Lumen! She and Nemo are playing just outside the seaweed bed.

Marlin is very happy to see them both. He is also relieved to be out of the seaweed bed.

'Time to go home, Nemo!'
They wave to Lumen and say goodnight.
Nemo smiles at Marlin and reaches out to grab his fin. They have both had enough adventures for one day!

Disney · PIXAR

UP

Badge Building

By

CYNTHIA VITALE

Illustrated by

THE DISNEY STORYBOOK ARTISTS

Russell loved collecting badges. There was just one tiny problem: there weren't enough! But that was about to change.

'Okay,' Campmaster Strauch began. 'Each troop has been asked to submit a new Wilderness Explorer badge idea and we'll hold a contest in two weeks.'

Russell's face lit up. A chance to earn a badge that he invented himself? He had to win this contest!

Russell couldn't wait to get started, but he also wasn't sure what kind of badge to design.

'What do you think?' Russell asked Carl and Dug later that day. 'There are so many choices. I could take care of a rescue animal or build a birdhouse or—'

Dug pushed a book over to Russell with his nose.

'Hmmm,' Russell said, looking at the book.

'Paleontology?'

'It means finding bones,' Carl explained.

'Ooh, bones!' Dug cried, panting happily. 'I know where bones are!'

Russell looked at Carl and shrugged. 'Okay, Dug,' he said. 'Paleontology it is!'

Russell started straight away on his new Wilderness Explorer badge idea. First, he did his research. He learned that looking for bones was called 'doing a dig' and that the bones were called 'fossils'. The next day, he learned what went into preparing for a dig. Finally, he was ready to stage his own dig.

'Okay, Dug,' Russell said. 'Lead the way.'

Dug led Russell and Carl to the local park. 'Here,' he said. 'Find the bone! Find the bone! Find the bone!'

'Ummm . . . Dug,' Russell started. 'Are you sure? This is a playground.'

Dug enthusiastically wagged his tail. 'Bones are here. I have found the bones.'

Russell still wasn't sure, but he decided to trust Dug. He and Carl carried their equipment over to a large oak tree and began to dig.

A few minutes later, Russell spotted something in the ground. 'Hey!' he shouted. 'Dug was right! There are bones here.'

Russell knelt down and brushed the dirt away. Ever so carefully, he pulled the bone from the ground.

'Dug!' he said. 'This isn't a fossil. This is one of your bones!'

Dug happily spun around in circles. 'I am a good tracker. I have found the bones!'

Carl laughed. 'Well, we did tell him we were looking for bones.'

Russell sat down on a bench and put his head in his hands. 'Now what am I going to do?' he asked. 'I can't dig up the whole city looking for fossils.'

Carl sat down next to Russell. 'No, probably not,' he said. 'Paleontology is a great idea for a badge, but maybe it should wait until you have the time to do it right. There must be something else you could try.'

Russell knew Carl was right. He may have lost some time, but he hadn't lost his determination to win. Now, he just needed to figure out a new badge.

Russell came up with idea after idea, but nothing seemed right.

Astronomy was interesting, but he didn't have time to properly track the stars.

He thought about farming or agriculture, but he couldn't raise livestock in the city. And besides, Dug had eaten all his seeds!

Russell considered building a robot, but all the robotics books were checked out of the library.

And detective work sounded exciting, but try as they might, Russell and Dug couldn't find anything to investigate!

'You know,' Carl said, 'maybe none of these are working because they don't mean anything to you. We've never solved a mystery or built a robot. But that,' he pointed at Russell's chocolate bar, 'is something we know you are interested in.'

'Mr Fredricksen, you're a genius!' Russell cheered. 'I love chocolate more than anything in the world!'

The next day, Carl introduced Russell and Dug to a local baker and chocolatier. 'This is Roger,' Carl said. 'He knows everything there is to know about chocolate . . . and he owes me a favour.'

Roger shook Russell's hand. Then he handed Russell and Carl their very own aprons and chefs' hats. 'You'll need these,' he said. 'Come on back. I hope you don't mind getting a little messy!'

All morning, Roger taught Russell about making chocolate. Russell learned that chocolate started out with a cocoa bean. The bean was roasted and crushed before being mixed with things like sugar, vanilla and milk. He even got to try mixing the ingredients together to make his own chocolate.

Then came the really fun part! Using the chocolate they had made together, Roger taught Russell, Carl and Dug how to make all sorts of different desserts, from chocolate cupcakes with chocolate frosting to chocolate cream pie.

Even better, Russell got to taste everything as they baked.

'No chocolate for me,' Dug said. 'Just bones.'

The next day was the contest. Russell looked around at his competition. Everyone had come up with great ideas!

There was a woodworking badge, a movie making badge and even a roller coaster design badge.

Finally, it was Russell's turn to present his badge.

'I call it the Chocolate Lover's badge,' he said. 'In order to earn it, you have to learn how chocolate is made, make your own batch and make three different chocolate desserts.'

'It certainly does look tasty!' Campmaster Strauch said.

Carl put his hand on Russell's shoulder. 'You did good,' he said.

Russell cut into a piece of chocolate pie and took a bite.

'Mmmmm, is that good!' he said. 'Thank you both for helping me.'

Just then, there was a cheer from across the room. The roller coaster badge had won!

Carl clapped Russell on the shoulder. 'I'm proud of you anyway, and you should be proud too.'

'You know, it's funny,' Russell said. 'All I wanted was to win, but now that I've lost, I don't feel so bad about it. I got to learn all about something I love with you and that's worth way more than winning a contest. Besides, building a roller coaster sounds like fun . . . I can't wait to earn that badge!'

Disney

Pinocchio

A Real Boy

By

ELIZABETH SCHAEFER

Illustrated by

THE DISNEY STORYBOOK ARTISTS

The sun was just beginning to rise over Pinocchio's little village. The moment he awoke, Pinocchio leapt out of bed and ran to look at himself in the mirror.

He laughed with joy when he saw his reflection. It hadn't been a dream. The Blue Fairy had made him a real boy!

He smelled a wonderful scent coming from the kitchen.

As he sniffed the air, Pinocchio felt a strange sensation: his mouth began to water. *Is this what being hungry feels like?* he wondered.

Pinocchio ran to the kitchen. There he saw his father, Geppetto, cooking a huge breakfast. There were eggs and pancakes and bacon, and sausage and porridge and orange juice, and toast and milk and muffins, and . . . Pinocchio stopped trying to name everything on the table.

Geppetto grinned when he saw Pinocchio. 'I wanted to cook you something special for your first breakfast, but I couldn't decide what to make,' he said. 'So I made everything!'

Pinocchio's stomach rumbled as he looked at all the food.

'Well, come on,' Geppetto said. 'Dig in!'

Pinocchio sat down and tried a bite of eggs. 'It's chewy!' he said, his mouth full. 'And soft. And . . . delicious!' Pinocchio tried a little bit of all the food Geppetto had made. Every bite tasted different from the last.

'This is wonderful,' Pinocchio said. 'Can we eat all day long?'

'Oh, no.' Geppetto laughed. 'We'll be much too busy for that. I have so much to show you.'

'Can we take the food with us?' Pinocchio asked.

'That's an excellent idea,' Geppetto said. 'We'll have a picnic!'

Geppetto packed a lunch, and he and Pinocchio left to explore the village.

The first thing Pinocchio noticed was how brightly the sun shone. He blinked as he left the dark cottage and walked into the sunshine. Its dazzling beams felt warm against his skin. Pinocchio and Geppetto made a game of running in and out of the shadows all the way to the edge of town. When Pinocchio jumped through the last shadow, he felt a strange sensation in his stomach. It was different from hunger. It was—*Hic*. Pinocchio's tummy flip-flopped and a strange sound came from his throat.

'What—*hic*—is going—*hic*—on?' Pinocchio asked. He was starting to get scared.

'Don't worry,' Geppetto said. 'It's just the hiccups.'

'Hiccups?' Pinocchio asked. 'Will they ever—*hic*—stop?'

Geppetto showed Pinocchio how to hold his breath until the hiccups went away.

Pinocchio wasn't sure he liked this new experience. He had been so busy thinking about how much fun being a real boy was, he hadn't stopped to think about all the things that could go wrong.

Pinocchio grew silent as he followed Geppetto. At first, the sun's warmth had felt nice. But now Pinocchio was hot and sweaty. His feet hurt. And his stomach felt as empty as it had before breakfast.

Pinocchio finally asked the question he was most concerned about: 'Are we there yet?'

Geppetto took Pinocchio's hand. 'It's just over this hill . . .'

The pair climbed higher until they saw a beautiful valley below them.

‘Race you to the swimming hole?’ Geppetto asked.

Pinocchio nodded and ran off before Geppetto could get ready.

Father and son ran down the hill and collapsed in a happy pile next to the lake’s edge.

‘Time for food!’ Pinocchio cheered.

Geppetto laughed and began unpacking the picnic basket.

Geppetto and Pinocchio spent the rest of the day at the swimming hole, playing in the water and fishing on the bank.

As they played, Geppetto told Pinocchio stories of the many times he had visited the lake as a young boy.

Pinocchio felt much better now that he had eaten and rested. The cool water was refreshing after their long walk from the village. Even when Pinocchio scraped his knee on one of the willow trees, he didn't get upset. He was starting to realise what an exciting place the world was.

As the sun began to set, Pinocchio noticed a new feeling. His eyelids felt heavy, as though he could barely keep his eyes open. Then he yawned.

'I'm tired,' Pinocchio said, surprised at the realisation.

'You've had quite a big day,' Geppetto said. 'Are you ready to go home?'

Pinocchio nodded, and Geppetto lifted him onto his shoulders. He carried Pinocchio towards their little house in the village.

Sitting on Geppetto's back, Pinocchio looked up into the night sky. Far above them shone the Wishing Star, twinkling brightly. Pinocchio realised that being a real boy was more complicated than he had imagined.

'Today was fun, Father,' Pinocchio said. 'But . . . it was hard, too.'

Geppetto nodded, thinking about what Pinocchio had said. 'That's what being alive is. It's sunlight and bacon and hiccups and scraped knees. Some of it will be scary, but I promise I'll be right there with you.'

Geppetto waited for Pinocchio to answer, but all he heard was the sound of soft snoring. Pinocchio was fast asleep!

Geppetto laughed. 'Enough speeches. It's time to get you to bed.'

Geppetto carried Pinocchio as gently as he could to bed. He fluffed up the pillow and then drew the blankets close under Pinocchio's chin.

'Goodnight, my boy,' Geppetto said, leaning in to kiss Pinocchio on the forehead.

'Today was a dream come true. I cannot wait to share another adventure with you tomorrow.'

DISNEY · PIXAR

INCREDIBLES 2

Sweet Dreams, Jack-Jack

By

MEREDITH RUSU

Illustrated by

GURIHIRU

Jack-Jack is a baby just like any other. Except his family has *Super* powers.

His dad can lift super heavy things.

His mum can stretch super long.

His sister can make super force fields, and his brother can run super fast.

Together, they're the Incredibles!

Jack-Jack doesn't have powers . . .

Or does he?

One night, Mr Incredible put Jack-Jack to bed. He read him a story.

'In the country of Nodoff, the Frubbers of Freep are all giving in to the sweet succor of sleep.'

Closed went the book. Out went the light. And Jack-Jack went to sleep.

Sweet dreams, Jack-Jack.

Mr Incredible tiptoed downstairs. But a little while later, he heard something strange.

Jack-Jack was out of his crib!

How did that happen?

Back upstairs they went. Mr Incredible read the story again.

Closed went the book. Out went the light. And Jack-Jack went to sleep once more.

Sweet dreams, Jack-Jack.

Mr Incredible tiptoed downstairs. He held his breath. He turned the corner . . . and there was Jack-Jack.

Watching television. Again.

Oh, well. If Mr Incredible couldn't keep Jack-Jack in his crib, they might as well watch television together.

They snuggled up on the sofa.

Soon, Mr Incredible was fast asleep. Jack-Jack was not asleep. He was watching a movie about a masked criminal robbing a jewellery store.

Suddenly, Jack-Jack heard a noise!

A raccoon was rummaging through the rubbish bin outside.

Jack-Jack looked at the masked robber on the television.

He looked at the raccoon.

He knew what he had to do.

Jack-Jack headed to the door . . . and passed right through!

He threw the rubbish back into the bin and closed the lid . . . with just a look!

Jack-Jack was going to stop that raccoon robber.

He fended off the raccoon.

SMACK!

The raccoon fought back.

WHAM!

Then Jack-Jack
got all fired up!

AHRRRRR!

Now the raccoon was angry. He put out Jack-Jack's fire.

The raccoon was certain he'd gotten away with his evil plan to raid the rubbish.

HEE, HEE, HEE.

But he was wrong!

Meanwhile, all the noise had woken up Mr Incredible. He came out just in time to see Jack-Jack multiply . . . into a bunch of little Jack-Jacks!

The raccoon was surrounded! That was finally enough to scare the sneaky bandit away.

Mr Incredible scooped up all the Jack-Jacks. They combined back into one sweet little baby.

'Jack-Jack, did you go through a locked door?' Mr Incredible asked in amazement. 'And you multiplied? You have powers! Aw, yeah!'

He rubbed noses with Jack-Jack.

'You're a Super Baby.'

Then Mr Incredible stopped smiling.

'You're a Super Baby . . . who can multiply . . . and pass through any solid surface. *Oh, no*. What are we going to tell Mummy?'

Jack-Jack giggled.

'Let's wait until morning.'

ZZZZZZZ

Sweet dreams, Jack-Jack.